I. Q., It's Time

Mary Ann Fraser

WALKER & COMPANY ✱ NEW YORK

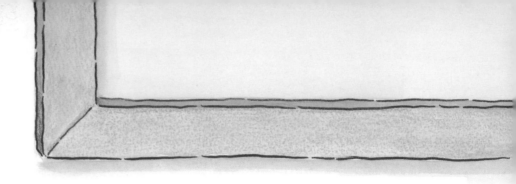

First published in the United States of America in 2005 by Walker Publishing Company, Inc.
Distributed to the trade by Holtzbrinck Publishers

For information about permission to reproduce selections from
this book, write to Permissions, Walker & Company, 104 Fifth Avenue, New York, New York 10011

Library of Congress Cataloging-in-Publication Data
available upon request
ISBN 0-8027-8978-1 (hardcover)
ISBN-13 978-0-8027-8978-5 (hardcover)
ISBN 0-8027-8980-3 (reinforced)
ISBN-13 978-0-8027-8980-8 (reinforced)

The artist used pencil, gouache, and pen and ink on Strathmore paper to create the illustrations for this book.

Book design by Victoria Allen

Visit Walker & Company's Web site at www.walkeryoungreaders.com

Printed in Hong Kong

2 4 6 8 10 9 7 5 3 1

To Barbara Swanson

At eight o'clock the bell rang.

I.Q. realized he was late for school. He was the class pet, but he really wanted to be a student.

SOAP

While Mrs. Furber, the teacher, took attendance, I.Q. quickly got ready. He finished just in time for the flag salute.

At eight fifteen Mrs. Furber said, "Class, today is going to be a busy day. Tonight is Parents' Night. We have to do our work *and* prepare the classroom. First we are going to practice telling time."

This gave I.Q. an idea. He would make a surprise for Parents' Night.

Mrs. Furber showed the children the teaching clock. "The big hand on the clock tells the minutes and the small hand tells the hours."

But I.Q. wasn't listening. He was looking for paper to make the surprise.

By the time I.Q. had found some paper it was nine o'clock, and Mrs. Furber needed his help for the science lesson.

"It takes the Earth twenty-four hours to spin around once," she said. "That is what we call a day."

I.Q. helped show how the Earth spins.

Then he showed how the Moon spins around the Earth. By the end of the lesson, I.Q.'s head was spinning, too.

He got some scissors to cut his piece of paper
into a circle for his project. He decided a paper plate
would be better. But before he could find one it was . . .

. . . ten o'clock, time for recess. Mrs. Furber passed out jump ropes.

I.Q.'s was too big. Stephanie gave him one that was more his size.

At ten thirty Mrs. Furber said, "We are going to make name cards, so tonight your parents will know where you sit."

I.Q. wanted to make sure the parents knew where he sat, too.

"It's eleven o'clock," said Mrs. Furber. "Time for math.
We are going to count by fives."

The class counted together.

"Each number on a clock stands for five minutes,"
said Mrs. Furber. "Can you match up the minutes with
the numbers?"

This reminded I.Q. that he still needed to finish his surprise for Parents' Night. He began writing numbers on little round stickers. I.Q. was only on number 5 when the bell rang, telling everyone it was . . .

. . . twelve noon.

"Lunch!" thought I.Q. He stood in line in the cafeteria, and Mr. Cook gave him a bowl of macaroni and cheese, I.Q.'s favorite. He was careful to save a paper plate for his project.

When he was done eating, I.Q. joined in a game of dodgeball. He had to dodge balls and feet. Mrs. Fields, the yard monitor, blew her whistle just in time.

Back in the classroom Mrs. Furber asked, "What time is it?"

I.Q. looked at the clock on the wall. The big hand was on the twelve and the small hand was on the one. One o'clock. He had six more hours to finish his surprise. But he couldn't work on it now. It was his favorite time of day.

I.Q. was the first one to the reading rug.

At two o'clock I.Q. still couldn't work on his surprise. Everyone had to go outside for PE.

Mrs. Jugar, the PE teacher, said, "Everyone line up. We are going to run races."

I.Q. borrowed the stopwatch. He timed the runners to see who was the fastest. He discovered that there were sixty minutes in an hour and sixty seconds in a minute. He also discovered that it took him three seconds to get across the track.

At two forty-five the school bell rang. As the children left, Mrs. Furber said, "I'm looking forward to meeting your parents tonight. Please remind them that Parents' Night is at seven o'clock."

I.Q. was very worried. It was three o'clock and he had a lot more to do on his surprise. The parents would be there in only four more hours.

He had just started working on his project when Mrs. Furber asked for his help.

By four o'clock they had finished hanging all of the students' work on the bulletin board and decorating the room.

I.Q. rummaged around for two strips of paper. He found just what he needed at the bottom of the wastepaper can. But once he was in, he couldn't find a way out.

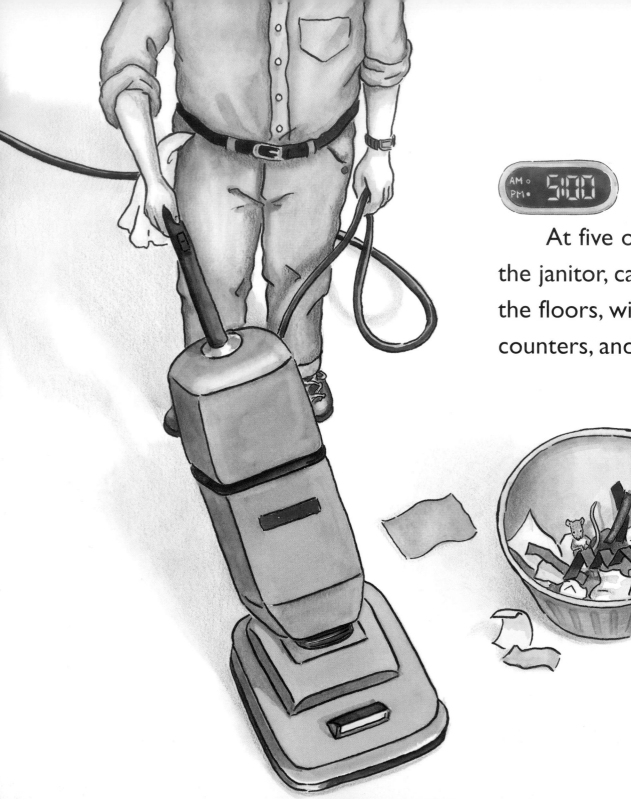

At five o'clock Mr. McBroom, the janitor, came in to vacuum the floors, wipe off the desks and counters, and empty the trash.

I.Q. escaped just in time. He studied the hands on the wall clock. It was . . .

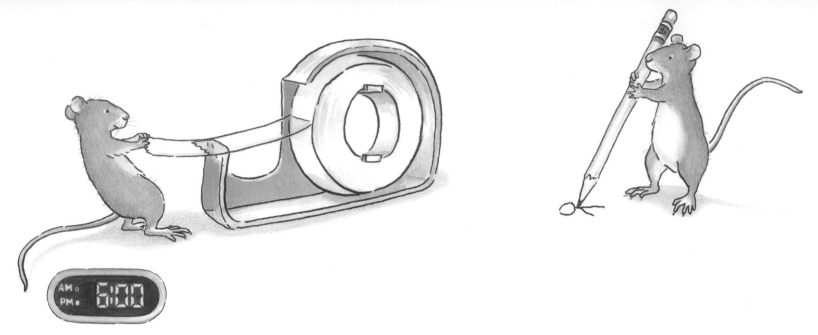

. . . six o'clock. Only one hour left before the parents would arrive.
He taped. He stapled. He pinned and drew. Whew! Finished at last.
Finally he was ready to show Mrs. Furber what he had made for
Parents' Night.

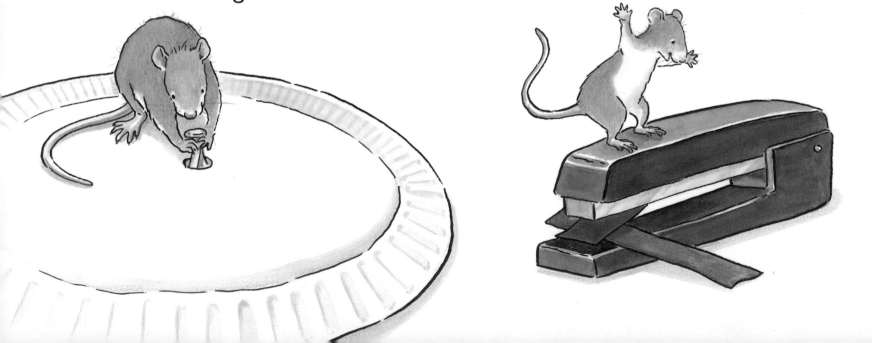

"Oh, I.Q.," she cried. "It's PERFECT!"

I.Q. pointed to Mrs. Furber's watch.

"You're right," she said, "it's time."

At seven o'clock Mrs. Furber let all of the parents into the classroom. "Welcome to Parents' Night," she said. "Come see what your children have been learning."

Some parents looked at the bulletin boards. Others found where their child sat.

When they discovered I.Q.'s surprise,
everyone wanted to know who had made it.

Mrs. Furber winked at I.Q. and replied, "One of our students."
I.Q. was very proud. Mrs. Furber had called him a student.

At eight o'clock all of the parents left, and
Mrs. Furber turned out the lights.

I.Q. yawned. Even though he could not see the
clock in the dark, he knew exactly what time it was.

It was time for bed.